THE ELEPHANT TREE

THE ELEPHANT TREE

Melanie Doré

Book Guild Publishing
Sussex, England

First published in Great Britain in 2013 by
The Book Guild Ltd
Pavilion View
19 New Road
Brighton, BN1 1UF

Typesetting in Palatino by
Nat-Type, Cheshire

Printed and bound in Great Britain by
CPI Group (UK) Ltd, Croydon, CR0 4YY

A catalogue record for this book is available from
The British Library.

ISBN 978 1 84624 890 0

For Charis and Josh,
my inspirations for writing this book, and in
memory of my mum.

Contents

New Beginnings

The journey from Norfolk to London seemed to be never-ending to Jessica. She gazed out of the car window, looking solemnly at the many cars her father passed as he drove at speed in the fast lane. The weather seemed to mirror her mood. The sky was dark and heavy and the rain had persisted for the whole of their journey.

She glanced down at the paperback lying next to her on the back seat of the car and tried to muster up enough enthusiasm to actually pick it up and read it.

She could remember when she first became disenchanted with escaping into make-believe. It all began when she started secondary school. She lost all enthusiasm for anything to do with her studies. She found it hard to settle in and make new friends. Then the bullying started and the last thing she wanted was to be called a geek. So in an attempt to try and make friends and fit in, she distanced herself from her studies and her reading. Not that it made any difference. She still couldn't quite find what she needed within herself to make the effort to be like the other girls, who were all into boys and make-up and stuff. She would try to join in, but they could all tell she was just bluffing when she tried to be interested in the boy of the moment or some new hairstyle. She liked a couple of the girls in her class at first, but soon realized that they were just like sheep – following the popular girls around and agreeing with anything they said just to keep in with them. That wasn't what she was like. She would rather be on her own than do that. 'Independent', that was what Mum said she was. Mum said it was a good thing, because she had a mind of her own and wouldn't just do or think the same as someone else. However, very occasionally she would find herself secretly wishing she could be the same as the other girls.

Still trying to find an excuse for not reading on the journey, she stared out of the window. They were just passing a road sign: 1 mile to go before they reached their destination. *Well*, she thought, *there's no point in picking the book up to read now, we'll be there in a minute.*

At the same moment Mum turned round with a smile and broke into her daughter's day-dreaming. 'Jess! JESS! We're nearly there, love. Emily, make sure you put your shoes on now, we'll be there soon.'

Jessica, who was twelve years old, was sitting next to her six-year-old sister Emily. They had been travelling for over two hours from their old house in

Norfolk to what was to be their new home in London. Emily was so excited about the prospect of living so close to central London and visiting all its famous sites that her eyes nearly popped out of her head when she saw the Wembley Arch in the distance. Jessica, on the other hand, was dreading having to start another school where she probably wouldn't make any friends and would be picked on yet again.

The two girls had only seen the house from a picture on the estate agent's details. Their mum and dad had preferred to choose the house on their own.

They turned off the main road and drove past lots of very smart Dutch-style chalet houses with long slanting roofs. Jess thought they looked rather higgledy-piggledy with their loft conversions and extensions. They turned left, then right, then left again.

'This is the road, girls,' Dad said. 'See if you can spot which one it is.'

As their dad drove slowly down the road, both girls wanted to wind down their windows to see the houses more clearly, but were stopped by the driving rain. Jessica didn't want to count the house numbers. She knew she would recognize theirs from the photo she had seen.

'It's on my side. I just know it is,' Jessica said. 'And there it is!'

'You're right!' announced her mum. 'Number 37.'

As Jessica peered out of the car window through the pouring rain, she examined the house. It looked like a typical, traditional family house, like the ones she had seen on the old black-and-white films she watched with her nan and granddad. It wasn't like the other Dutch-style ones in the neighbouring roads. This one didn't have a long sloping roof. Instead it stood proud and upright. She remembered her dad saying it was built in the 1930s like the other houses in that area. But how dishevelled and run down it looked compared to the houses on either side! The window frames were rotten in parts, the paint flaking off. The house was a dirty cream colour and the front garden was overgrown with dead or dying plants.

The rain was coming down harder than ever. Once Mum had found the front door key, they all decided to jump out of the car quickly and make a run for the front porch. Mum and Jess were the first two out of the car. Holding their jackets over their heads, they pushed open the rickety old gate and ran up the garden path, trying to dodge the overgrown clumps of grass.

Jess reached the front door just as Mum was opening it. The door was a dark green colour with a semicircle of stained glass set into it, yellow and clear glass in a sun-ray pattern.

4

As they walked inside she immediately noticed an old, slightly musty, yet lightly perfumed smell. It reminded Jessica of old roses, but she didn't dislike it. She moved around the many boxes the removal men had left stacked up in the hall the day before.

Jess and Emily had stayed with their grand-parents near Cambridge the previous night, while their parents had helped the removal men unload. Jessica thought how different this house was from their old one, which had been more modern but somehow had less charm.

Emily and Dad came bursting into the house, laughing loudly at themselves for getting so wet just running from the car to the front door.

'Wow! Look at all those boxes! Have we got to unpack all of those today?' exclaimed Emily.

'No, not all of them right away,' replied Mum. 'Just the ones we need to have now.'

'Can we help?' Emily asked.

'Yes, of course you can! How about sorting out the boxes for your rooms?'

'Our new bedrooms!' squealed Emily. 'Let's go and find our new bedrooms, Jess! Can we choose which we have?'

'No way!' said Jess firmly. 'After Mum and Dad's room, I automatically get the next biggest and you get the box room.'

'That's not fair!' Emily was suddenly angry. 'Why do I always have to get the smallest room?'

'Just the way it is, I'm afraid, Em. You're the youngest,' said Dad calmly. 'I always had to have the smallest room too, because Uncle James was the oldest. Anyway, it's cool sometimes because it's cosier and you get one of those beds with a den underneath.'

'I'll race you, little sis!' called Jess.

She reached the landing first and burst through the door opposite the top of the stairs. Even though the room was full of boxes and furniture, she could tell that it was a big, square room.

Emily ran in a moment later, shouting, 'This is my room!'

'No it isn't, silly!' said Jessica sarcastically. 'How can it be when it's got all *my* furniture and stuff in it?'

'Where's my room?' shouted Emily to her parents.

'Yours is one of the others!' they shouted back, laughing.

Emily looked into one of the two rooms at the front of the house. 'Wow! Is this really huge one mine?'

'No! Nice try … Go into the smaller one!'

Emily ran into the room next door. 'Wow!' she shouted again. 'It's got a special window!'

Dad finally climbed the stairs to join her. 'Yes, it's

called an oriel window,' he said as he picked her up and sat her on the windowsill so she could look out.

'Still raining!' she said.

'Yes,' he sighed.

Jessica looked around her room, trying to decide how she was going to arrange all the furniture. Then she noticed the wallpaper. It was patterned with pretty pink roses, a bit faded. Although it looked old, she liked it. Her thoughts turned to whoever might have lived there before. Maybe an old married couple? No, that didn't feel right. Somehow she just knew that it was an old lady who had lived on her own.

Just then her dad came in and said, 'How do you like your new room?'

'It's great,' Jess told him. 'Much bigger than my old one, and I really like the wallpaper. Can I keep it for a while, Dad?'

'No problem, of course you can. It will be a while before we get round to decorating upstairs anyway. There's so much else to do first.'

Just as he turned to walk out of the room, Jess asked, 'Dad, who owned the house before we did?'

'An old lady,' he said. 'She apparently lived here on her own and never married. So she had no children and no one to leave the house to.'

How sad, Jess thought.

She walked over to the window and looked out at the back garden. How overgrown and neglected it looked! She examined what she could see of the surrounding gardens, and realized that their own looked bigger. Even though it was a mess, she could tell that it was much longer and slightly wider than the others. There were also several large trees, one of which she couldn't see properly as it was obscured by another. However, she thought she could just make out something in the tree – something large, poking out a bit to the side. She moved her head closer to the window and narrowed her eyes. But it was no good. She couldn't see clearly enough. She would have to wait until the rain had stopped and she could go out into the garden for a closer look.

That night after tea, which was a takeaway of fish and chips because they had no food in the house and couldn't find the pots and pans anyway, Jess went up to her room and started to sort out some of the many boxes. She finished one and decided to start on another that had been placed up high on a chest of drawers. She knew that some of her cuddly toys were in there and it wouldn't be heavy.

She found the stool to her dressing table and stood on top of it. As she pulled the box towards her, she noticed that there was a door hidden behind all the furniture and boxes. It must belong to a built-in cupboard. Curious to find out what, if anything, was in there, she shouted for her dad with urgency in her voice.

Dad came rushing breathlessly upstairs. 'What's up? What's so important? I was just in the middle of moving some rather heavy boxes. Are you OK?'

'I'm fine, Dad. It's just that I've found a cupboard behind my chest of drawers and I want to see inside. There might still be stuff in there left behind from the lady who used to live here.'

'Well,' sighed Dad, 'it'll have to wait until I've finished what I'm doing downstairs. It's getting late and we've all had a long, busy day. Why don't you get ready for bed? I'll be up shortly to move those things. Anyway, there probably won't be anything of value in there.' He gave her a little wave and stumped back down the stairs.

Jess emptied her box of cuddly toys on the bed, sorted them out and arranged some of them on her large wooden bookshelf and some of them on her windowsill, keeping one rather old and scruffy-looking dark brown bear on her bed to cuddle later. She got undressed and climbed into bed.

A knock sounded on her door. 'It's just me come to say goodnight,' said her dad. 'Mum will be up in a minute.'

'Are you going to move those boxes, Dad?'

'Not tonight. I'm too tired and they can wait till morning.'

'Oh Dad, you promised!'

'It's too late for you to go rummaging through a dirty old cupboard now. I'll move them first thing after breakfast tomorrow, OK?'

Jess was disappointed. 'OK,' she sighed.

'Are you going to be all right sleeping in your new room, or would you like a light on?' asked her dad.

'I'm not a kid, Dad! I'll be fine,' she retorted.

'OK, just asking.' Her dad leant over to give Jess a goodnight kiss on her forehead.

After her dad had left the room, Jess got out of bed and peered round the other end of the chest of drawers which was near the wall. She realized the gap was just big enough for her to squeeze alongside the chest and get behind it. Could she open the door to the cupboard enough to see inside? She could!

Frustration. *Great*, she thought sarcastically. *It's too dark! I need my torch, but it's still packed somewhere.* She decided to be brave and put her hand inside the dark cupboard to have a feel around. She felt nothing at first, but waved her arm about a bit and slowly moved downwards at the same time until she was in a kneeling position. She was just about to give up when her fingers brushed against something positioned behind the door. But she

10

couldn't reach any further in. She would have to leave it till morning after all.

As Jess squeezed back alongside the chest of drawers she heard her mum coming up the stairs. Not wanting to get into trouble for not being in bed, she leapt across the room and jumped into bed, turning the light off on the way. When her mum came in, she lay still and pretended to be asleep. She heard her mum creep out and carefully shut the door, and then started to imagine what could be in that mysterious cupboard. However, tiredness soon overcame her and it was not long before she was genuinely fast asleep.

Exploring

Jess woke late the next morning. The first thing she heard was her sister shouting as she passed Jess's bedroom door. As she tried to concentrate on what Emily was saying, she forced her eyes open. She had forgotten to close her curtains the night before, so the brilliant morning sunshine was streaming through the window and onto her bed. The brightness made her eyes hurt at first, but as she acclimatized it dawned on her that it was no longer raining and that they could play outside and explore the garden.

It appeared that Emily had slept in too and had to have breakfast first. So Jess ran into the bathroom, got herself ready and joined Emily at the breakfast table. It was while Jess was munching through her cereal that she remembered the cupboard in her room.

'Dad, can you move my chest and things today? Pleeease!'

'Yes, of course. I'll move them in a minute.'

After Jess and Emily had finished their breakfast, they rushed off to find their shoes while their dad went up to move Jess's chest of drawers.

The girls ran excitedly out into the garden to explore. Jess was keen to see what was poking out of the side of the big tree. They both ran down through the very overgrown grass, with its long wet blades brushing against their legs and making them wish they had worn wellies. Jess stopped halfway down the garden at the tree, while Emily ran right down to the end. Jess just stood still, looking up at the massive tree before her. Emily came rushing back and stopped next to Jess, following her sister's gaze. What was she looking at?

'*Wow!*' cried Emily. 'It's a tree house! It's a tree house! It's a tree house!' She jumped up and down, whooping with excitement.

'Yes, isn't it brilliant!' said Jess.

Emily's cries brought their parents outside to see what was going on.

'What's all the noise about?' they asked.

The girls both shouted out at the same time, 'We have a tree house!'

'Oh, so you found the beech tree! We thought we'd keep it as a surprise until we got here and let you discover it yourselves.'

Jess looked up at the impressive tree that held the rather tatty old tree house. With its outstretched branches that looked like arms and its dark red leaves and grey bark, she thought how majestic it looked standing there, its leaves gently swaying in the breeze. She transferred her gaze to the tree house. Although it had clearly seen better days, she couldn't wait to climb up and sit in it.

'When can we play in it, Dad?' she asked.

'Well, I need to do some work on it first to make sure it's safe.'

'Can you do it today, please, Dad?' Emily pleaded.

'Listen, girls, I can't do it today. I already have a million other jobs to do in the house!'

'Dad, if you fix it soon we can play in it all over the summer holidays and we'd be keeping out from under your feet. Please, Dad!' said Jess.

'She's got a point,' Mum put in.

Dad gave Mum a 'thanks very much, I thought you were supposed to be on my side' look.

'Let me think about it. Anyway, I've moved everything out of the way of that cupboard in your room, Jess, and I've put everything I found in there on your bed.'

'Brilliant. Thanks, Dad.'

Jess dashed back up the garden, through the house and up the stairs, two at a time. Running into her bedroom, she saw two boxes and one brown leather suitcase on her bed. The suitcase looked intriguing. But as much as she wanted to open that, she decided to resist temptation and save the best till last. She carefully opened the lid of the top box, dislodging the dust which made her cough. Her heart sank a little as she peered inside. *Old newspapers, only old newspapers*, she thought.

Not really sure what she had expected to find in the boxes, she decided to take the papers out. After she had taken out the top two or three, she realized they were all newspapers from special dates. There were several from the millennium and one of the Mars *Beagle* lander. There were a couple from when Princess Diana and Prince Charles got married and quite a few from the Queen's Silver Jubilee. Some dated right back to before the Americans landed on the moon in 1969.

After putting the newspapers carefully away, she turned her attention to the large brown suitcase. She unlocked both ends of the case and lifted the lid. Inside there were what looked like lots of hardback books, all similar in style. *Boring! Just what I've always wanted ... books!* she thought gloomily. She lifted out one from the top and opened it up. She flicked through the book, expecting to find pages of typed words, but instead found herself looking at pages of handwritten text. These weren't books. They were diaries!

She started to read a page at random, but found it hard to understand without knowing the context. She needed to start at the beginning. The hand-writing was different from hers and her mum's. She thought it looked old-fashioned, like the way her nan and granddad might write. Then she noticed the date on the top of the page – 12 June 1943. *These are really old!* she thought. And there were loads of them. She also noticed that inside each book, on the first page, the letters 'ET' were written, along with some numbers: ET 35, ET 15, ET 40. She tried to work out what it meant. Was it something to do with aliens, like the film *ET*?

Suddenly her interest was aroused. She took all the books out to find the one with the earliest date. Skimming through the pages, she glanced out of the window. She could hear Emily pretending to climb up the tree to the tree house. However, she couldn't quite see her sister, so lost interest and continued to look through the diaries.

Outside, Emily was trying her hardest to climb up the beech tree. As she had a go from every angle, she was squashing the long blades of grass that grew up and around the base of the tree. After a while she became bored with her failure to get a grip on the trunk and moved away. But as she did so, she noticed something odd …

Upstairs, Jess picked up the last of the books, still looking for the one with the earliest date. She turned it over and opened it up to the first page. Inside she saw the date – 28 June 1938. That one had to be the earliest.

She could hear her sister shouting outside and becoming very excited about something. Then she heard her mum and dad talking and laughing with Emily. Curious, she got up, dropped the opened book on the bed and turned to look out of the window. What were they looking at?

She opened the window and called out to them. 'What's the matter? What are you looking at?'

'Guess what I've found!' Emily shouted.

'What?'

'An elephant foot!'

'What do you mean? How can there be an elephant's foot in our garden, silly?'

Dad intervened before there could be an argument. 'What Em means is, the base of our beech tree looks exactly like an elephant's foot. Come and have a look!'

'Yes,' said Emily defiantly, 'that's what I mean. We have a base of a tree that looks like an elephant's foot. Hey, we could call it the Elephant Tree!'

Just then, Jess turned around to see that the diary had fallen open to another page to reveal the words of a heading: 'The Elephant Tree'. The penny dropped. That was what 'ET' stood for – 'Elephant Tree'. Then the diaries were probably written by someone who had lived in the house a long time

17

ago; maybe the old lady who had lived here before they did. It was all making sense to Jess.

She quickly ran down to join her family in the garden to see the elephant tree. It was amazing. Now she could see that the tree trunk was exactly the same colour as an elephant. The bark had formed into crinkly lines which looked like the wrinkles on the skin of an elephant. At the very bottom of the tree there were patches of lighter coloured bark in semicircle shapes. There were some missing and they were roughly shaped, but at a distance they did resemble an elephant's toenails.

Not wanting to tell the rest of her family about her find yet, Jess ran back inside to her bedroom. With curiosity getting the better of her, she picked up the first of the diaries and began to read.

The memoirs of Peggy Forester, age 12

I am the eldest of 3 children. My younger sister Kitty is 8 and my little brother Jack is 5. My mother's name is Elizabeth and my father's name is Ernest. My father is a lawyer and until recently worked alongside his father at his practice. My father is a very clever man. My mother says he is well respected as a lawyer and a man. However he would never boast about himself or his achievements as he is also a true gentleman. To me though, he is just about the best father anyone could have. When he's with us children he plays just like he's a big child himself. He works hard but always has time for us.

My beautiful mother used to be a teacher until I came along. She gave up teaching to bring up her three children. I think she always intended to teach in between having children, but never got around to it, saying that having us three was enough to keep her happy and contented. Although Jack is now 5 and will be starting school soon, I think that Mother wants to start working again, maybe in a school nearby. My mother is a truly lovely person, very kind, patient, loving and giving. She is beautiful too, tall and slender with long wavy fair hair. Some say she resembles a movie star. Everyone who meets her loves her. Like my father who said it was love at first sight. You can tell they are still very much in love and as happy today as they were when they first met.

Not much to tell you about my sister other than that she is just very annoying and I wish that I didn't have to share a room with her. Also I wish she would just go away and leave me alone. Well, sometimes anyway.

My brother, well, you just can't help loving him. He's got that same something about his

19

personality that my mother has. Everyone loves him. He's a real character, cheeky and funny and very daring for his age, always causing my mother to gasp with fear and her heart to miss a beat. All this, though, just adds to his strong but lovable personality.

It was my father's idea for me to start a diary because I love to write. Stories mainly, but I just love writing anything. I didn't want to call it a diary, so my mother suggested I called it my 'memoirs'. I think this is a much better idea because a diary sounds so childish and after all, next birthday I will be 13 years old, so I'm not a little child any more. 'Memoirs' sounds much more grown up.

I'm not sure who will want to read my memoirs, if anyone, but my father said that maybe when I'm an old lady my children or my grandchildren may want to read them. He said that writing about my life now will be like taking a photograph, freezing time for the reader in the future. By me writing about how my life is today, I will be making a permanent record for whoever reads it in the future. He said that maybe one day I could publish them. I know he was only kidding really, but that is my dream to have something that I have written published.

28 June 1938

I have chosen now to start my memoirs because today is the day we have moved into our new house and I thought this was the perfect time.

The house is only two years old. My father inherited it from his Uncle Harold. Unfortunately, Uncle Harold only lived here for about 18 months before he died and he moved into it when it was new. His plan was to live out the rest of his years in one of the new-build homes in comfort. He was a relatively poor man most of his life, only making his fortune a few years before he died. I overheard my father saying it was by 'dubious means' in investments over in America. Once he'd made his fortune, Uncle Harold came back to England to be closer to the only family he had – us. It's such a shame he didn't live longer to enjoy his new house, but I suppose in a way he did live his last years in comfort, though there weren't very many of them.

It's a very posh house and a fine neighbourhood compared to where we lived before, and the rooms are much bigger. My brother has a room to himself, being the only boy, and I have to share with my sister again. Still, it's such a lovely house with its stained-glass windows, and Mother has a much larger pantry and larder, I'm sure she won't know where she is.

Then there's the garden. It's so enormous my brother called it a playing field when he first saw it, but then we only had a tiny garden before, which was Mother's pride and joy. She spent many hours tending and nurturing it and transforming a small area of plain and uninteresting grass into a beautiful cottage-style rose garden. She has already set her sights on the front garden and a small patch of border where the fence is for a climbing rose to trail along.

However, I haven't yet got to the most interesting part about the garden and what makes this house the best one in the street. When we were exploring the back garden, we found the most delightful surprise. The garden has a beech tree which has an unusual base to its trunk. Well, I can only describe it as though we've got one leg and a foot of an elephant standing in our garden! When my brother saw it he said maybe the other three legs of the elephant were in the other back gardens. It's because of this we decided to call it 'The Elephant Tree' ...

Jess felt as though she was discovering her new house and the elephant tree for the first time along with Peggy, closing the gap of the many years that lay between them. She became so absorbed by Peggy's diary that she felt like she was actually there. In her imagination she could clearly see them all, as if she was seeing it through Peggy's eyes. Imagining she could hear their voices and could almost touch them. All the sights, sounds and smells of Peggy's story came to life in Jess's imagination.

Moving In

Lying on her back on the grass, hands behind her head, Peggy gazed up at the almost clear blue sky on that flaming hot day in June. As she studied the horsetail clouds in the sky, she seemed oblivious to the noise and chaos around her. Her brother Jack and her sister Kitty were running around her in the back garden playing chase, her mother and father were going back and forth in and out of the house, carrying boxes and pieces of furniture along with two burly removal men. It was only when Jack tripped over her leg and fell on her that she snapped out of her day-dreaming.

'Ouch! That hurt, Jack. Your shoe buckle's caught my ankle and made it bleed!'

'Sorry, Peggy, it was an accident.'

Not being able to be mad at Jack for long, she forgave him. 'It's all right.' Rubbing her ankle, she sat up properly and looked around at their new garden.

There seemed to be very few flowers. *Well*, she thought, *it won't stay like that for long once Mother gets stuck in.* Sitting with her legs pulled up to her chest and arms folded around them, she let her eyes wander around the garden. Suddenly, she saw the beech tree. Surprised with herself at not noticing it sooner, she stood up and slowly walked towards the tree, surveying its shape as she got closer.

She started at the top, studying its copper-red leaves and the shape of the branches, following its form down to the top of the trunk. Its branches at this point were outstretched, reminding her of a mother's arms ready to hug her child. She moved her eyes downwards towards the base of the trunk and immediately noticed the strong resemblance to an elephant's foot. Standing in front of the tree, her fingertips caressing the rough ridges of the bark, she called for Jack and Kitty to come and see. 'Look, it's amazing!' she said.

They all stood looking down at the base of the tree, feeling its rippled bark. Jack gave a crow of delight and started to try and climb up the trunk.

'Careful, Jack, you might fall.'

'No I won't! I want to climb up to those big branches and sit on them.'

'There'll be no climbing trees today,' insisted a voice from behind the three children. Their father, hands in pockets, had come to see what his three children were getting up to. 'Mum sent me out to tell you to go and wash your hands ready for lunch.'

'Dad, look at this tree trunk. It looks like the foot of an elephant!' said Peggy.

Her father moved to get a closer look. 'So it does. I've never really noticed it before on my visits to see Uncle Harold.' He bent down and rubbed his hands over the bark. 'That's pretty amazing.'

'Can we build a tree house, Dad?' Jack asked excitedly.

'Yes, please, Dad!' both Peggy and Kitty pleaded.

'Like the one in the *Swiss Family Robinson* story,' Jack continued.

'I think the size of that one might be a bit too adventurous, Jack. Hmmm. Maybe something a bit smaller,' their father muttered as he examined the tree.

'Time for lunch!' called their mother from the kitchen window.

All three of the children ran up the garden and through the house. Both Kitty and Jack kept running until they got upstairs to wash their hands. Peggy, however, stopped abruptly just inside the French doors to the dining room. She stood with her mouth slightly open, looking at the interior of the room. The fireplace was the first thing she noticed, a typical art deco fire surround, with its geometric shape and tapered mantelpiece. Inlaid into the design was a semicircle of tiles that looked like golden marble. Every so often wavy red lines resembling flames were placed round the arch. It reminded her of a picture she had seen in a book of Japanese art. Inserted in the centre was a small square clock with a metal frame.

As she looked around the room, she discovered something they hadn't had in their old house: an electric light. Standing underneath it, she studied the marbled green lamp hanging above her. She looked around for the switch and spied it by the door. She couldn't resist running over and switching the light on and off – instant light; no more gas lamps and candles!

The rest of the house was equally interesting to Peggy. As she investigated, she found many of her Uncle Harold's possessions mixed in with their own. On the windowsill of the living room stood a bronze statuette of a slender lady. She stood with her arms stretched straight above her head and her body slightly arched backwards. In her hands she held a ball. Peggy noticed how her hair was cut in a short bob which she thought looked very modern and chic. Sitting on a side table there was a beautiful looking lamp. The cone-shaped lampshade was made out of different pieces of coloured glass, red, yellow and green all put together to resemble flowers. It had a slender bronze stand which opened out to what Peggy thought looked like a flat upside-down mushroom. However, her favourite piece of all was the clock on the mantle in the dining room. It was mainly made out of wood and the shape reminded Peggy of Napoleon's hat. Its face took up most of the middle part of the clock. However, the best bit of all was that it sounded just like Big Ben when it chimed. Peggy thought how many lovely things he had!

After lunch Peggy returned to the garden, this time with a pen and pencil, some plain paper and her new diary. She opened up the book to the first page and began by writing an introduction to herself and her family. To begin with she sat under the beech tree to keep out of the hot summer sun. However, after a while she tired of that and decided to move. Lying on her stomach opposite the beech tree, hands on her chin, she gazed at the tree's beautiful form. It was then that she decided to put pen to paper and draw the tree in all its glory. She spent the rest of the day and into the evening sketching and writing about the events of their first day in their new home in her new diary.

Making Friends

The next day Peggy sat on the wall outside the front of the house. As she sat looking down at her feet swinging back and forth below her, she became aware of children's voices and laughter. She looked up and turned her head towards the sounds of children playing. At the end of the road she saw two boys kicking a ball about to each other. Just then three girls came out of one of the houses with a skipping rope. It reminded her of her old friends where she used to live and how much she missed them. She felt sad and lonely. Then she remembered that she had to start a new school and she started to have that dreadful sinking feeling you get when you have to do something that you don't want to do. She turned her attention back to the children playing down the street and wished she had enough nerve to go and join in.

After a few minutes two ladies came out of the same house and walked towards her, talking and laughing loudly. As they approached Peggy's house, they stopped talking and smiled at her. One of them was carrying a large cake tin.

The larger of the two ladies said, 'Hello there, deary. I'm Mary and this is Dot. We live next door to each other down the road and we're your new neighbours. Saw you moving in yesterday and thought we'd bake you a cake as a welcoming gift. It's about time we came and introduced ourselves. Is your mother or father about?'

'Yes, they're both inside. I'm Peggy, by the way.'

Peggy led the way indoors, where the adults all exchanged names and stories about moving in and other neighbours in the street. Peggy's mum Elizabeth made a pot of tea and they all sat round eating cake, drinking tea and chatting.

When they had finished they all took a walk outside in the garden. Mary noticed the unusual beech tree and Jack blurted out that their dad was going to build a tree house. Ernest explained hastily that he hadn't planned on doing it just yet, as it would take a fair amount of work and they already had plenty of things to do inside the house. All three of his children's faces dropped when he announced his plans.

Mary saw how disappointed all the children were so came up with a clever idea.

'Why don't you let my Stan help you build it? After all, he is a carpenter. I know he won't mind, he's good like that, anything to help you all settle in. Anyway, you wouldn't want three miserable children hanging around all summer getting under your feet because they're bored,' Mary said smiling and giving Peggy, Kitty and Jack a wink.

Both Elizabeth and Ernest looked at each other; how could they refuse a generous offer like that?

'Well, if you are sure Stan won't mind then we would love to accept your very kind offer,' said Elizabeth.

'Well, that's settled then.'

Peggy could hardly contain her excitement. Grinning from ear to ear she said, 'Thank you so much, Mary, and thank Stan for us too.'

Peggy started to feel less anxious about settling in. A good feeling came over her and deep down she felt that she was going to like living here. The loneliness that she had felt before started to fade.

They had been chatting for nearly an hour when there was a knock at the door. Mary gasped. She rushed to the door, exclaiming, 'That'll be my brood wondering where I've got to. I clean forgot the time!'

The adults all followed her to the door. Peggy, although curious to meet whoever was on the other side of the door, stepped back to stand just inside the dining room, peeping around the door frame. Jack and Kitty, also feeling a bit shy, decided to sit halfway up the stairs and observe from there.

When the door was opened, they saw not one face, but many. It was the girl standing at the front

31

that Peggy noticed first. She was obviously the eldest. She was tall and slim with fine facial features. Her shoulder-length hair was tawny brown and wavy, pinned back at one side with a pretty butterfly clip.

Standing to one side was another girl, slightly shorter, with a much fuller face than the other girl. Her straight dark brown hair was cut short in a bob style. She had a pale complexion and piercingly blue eyes. Peggy could tell immediately that she was the daughter of Dot. Standing slightly behind her was another girl looking exactly like her, only younger. She was probably about Kitty's age, perhaps eight or nine.

Behind them Peggy noticed the face of a boy. He was obviously shorter than the girls as he was jumping up and down to try to get a better look. Between the jumps Peggy could see that he had fair hair, a round face and freckles. Last of all, Peggy noticed a face peering between the eldest girl's legs. It was the face of a boy no older than three. He looked quite similar to the jumping boy, but his face was chubbier and his hair was very blond, almost white. He was standing looking straight at Peggy with an extremely cheeky grin, making it very hard for her not to smile back.

As Peggy tried to match up the children to the parents, Mary introduced them all. The eldest girl and two boys were Mary's. The girl was called Rosie and the biggest boy Freddie. As for the boy with an irresistible grin, he was called Teddy. Mary explained that actually his real name was Frank, but from the time he could crawl he had made a beeline for Rosie's favourite bear, Baxter, and his first word hadn't been 'mummy' or 'daddy', but 'teddy'. The two girls with identical bobs were Dot's daughters Madeline and Evie, the youngest being Evie.

Peggy glanced nervously over at the eldest boy as he jumped up, secretly wanting to join them with their games outside. Only, being shy, she didn't feel able to make the first move and invite herself into their group.

She didn't have to. Before she knew it, Mary was bustling over to her. 'Now Peggy,' she said cheerfully, 'you, Kitty and Jack mustn't be shy! Come and join our lot outside now and play for a while. It'll give your parents time to get on without all of you getting under their feet!' Everyone laughed and it wasn't long before all eight children were outside playing and Peggy, Kitty and Jack were making new friends.

The Tree House

In the days and weeks that followed, the children patiently watched a few planks of wood change into a proper little house, complete with a wooden ladder that went from the ground up to a trap door in the floor of the tree house for them to climb through.

It was Peggy who showed the most interest in the tree house, wanting to help design and build it. Freddie also showed a great interest, but no one could quite work out whether it was the tree house, Peggy or both he liked to visit. It was obvious from the start that he liked Peggy and the feeling seemed to be mutual. They became great friends.

The tree house was finished as the summer started. All the children had been planning a party for the grand opening. Peggy decided to put herself in charge as she was the eldest. She assigned Jack to making paper chains and Kitty to colouring and cutting out small triangles to attach to some string to make bunting. On the day she would make cakes and her mother sandwiches.

The night before the party she fell asleep thinking about the great day. No sooner had she closed her eyes, it seemed, it was morning and Jack was jumping on her bed shouting, 'Peggy, get up! It's party day! Peggy, *wake up!*'

The sun was shining. It was going to be another glorious summer day. Peggy, who was as excited about the day as Jack, leapt out of bed and rushed to get ready.

Madeline, Evie and their parents were the first to arrive. Peggy opened the door to them. 'Come through to the garden!' she said, and followed on behind the girls' father, Eric Potts. He was a rather tall, thin man who walked with a limp. Her mother had told her it was because he'd had an accident at work a few years earlier. Mr Potts was an architect and he had designed some of the houses in their road, including the one he and his family lived in. The Potts' house was at the end of the road on the corner and had a much larger garden than many of the other houses. It also boasted a lovely low slanting roof with a cute little window that looked like an eye peeping out. It was enchanting. Apparently he had been inspecting one of the building sites when he had fallen from the top floor of a house. He was lucky to be alive, but it had left him with a limp. He was a gentle man with a kind but sad face, which Peggy thought was maybe a result of frustration that he couldn't do as much as he could before the accident.

Soon after the Potts arrived, the Arnolds were knocking at the door. Mary came first, bustling past Kitty, fretting that she was going to drop the fruitcake because she was carrying far too much. It looked like she was prepared to feed an army!

They all walked through to the garden, where Peggy and everyone else had already congregated. Freddie made a beeline for Peggy and from behind his back produced a bunch of yellow roses. 'For you,' he announced.

Peggy, taken by surprise, stood momentarily with her mouth wide open, not saying a word. The brief moment of silence was broken by Freddie's dad, who jokingly said, 'Freshly picked this morning from next door's garden!'

'Oh, Stan,' scolded Mary. 'You know that's not true! Don't believe a word of it, Peggy my love. They come from our bush out the back.'

Feeling rather silly, with everyone's attention on him, Freddie explained hastily, 'They're for the tree house. To brighten it up.'

The other children all looked at each other, trying not to snigger. Then Jack said quite innocently what everyone else was thinking but trying hard not to say, 'Freddie loves Peggy!'

The other children all burst out laughing, making Peggy and Freddie go bright red.

'Opening ceremony,' said Peggy's mum firmly, coming to the rescue.

After the cutting of the ribbon, which Kitty and Jack held and Peggy cut, the party got under way and the children eagerly climbed the steps to the tree house to get their first glimpse. The sun shone brightly in the clear blue sky while the children played either in the tree house or around the garden.

After a while Peggy tired of playing Catch and It with the others and took her diary up to the tree house to sketch and write about the day so far. Being up high, looking down on everyone, gave her an unusual perspective and the advantage of being able to draw people without them knowing. It meant she could study their features and mannerisms and capture the essence of who they were. While she sketched her mind wandered, thinking ahead to the many other days they could all spend together, playing in the tree house and at each other's houses and out in the street like a gang. It felt like it would never end. She had an overwhelming feeling of safety and belonging.

As the day finally came to an end and the sun disappeared over the horizon, the Potts and the Arnolds decided it was time to take their children home. Tired but happy, the children said their goodbyes. Peggy decided to take one last look out of the tree house on its first day. She felt that the tree house was very much hers, although she knew it belonged to all of them really. Already it felt like a special place.

A Confidence

In the weeks and months that followed, the tree house became almost like a second home, not only for Peggy, Kitty and Jack, but also for Freddie, Madeline and Evie. Teddy was judged too small to climb the ladder safely, much to his frustration, and he always protested loudly when he visited with his mum, brother and sister. He was desperate to be a part of the group's activities and games that went on in the tree house. As for Rosie, she felt it was mostly for kids to play in and wasn't prepared to risk laddering her tights to climb up the ladder and into the tree house. But for the rest it became the place to be and, without any of the children noticing, apart from Peggy, it helped the group's friendships to deepen. From tea parties with their favourite dolls and bears to relaxing on a sunny Sunday afternoon, the little wooden house perched high in the tree was transformed into a place of adventure and fantasy.

It was also a place for the group to share their secrets, wishes and dreams. Late one afternoon, while Peggy was sitting sketching in her diary, Rosie paid her and the tree house a surprise visit.

Peggy, who was sitting looking out of the window in between writing and sketching in her diary, heard someone climbing the ladder. Thinking it was probably either Kitty or Jack, she didn't bother to look round. So when she heard Rosie's voice, she was totally amazed.

At first Peggy didn't know what to say. However, she soon realized that Rosie must have something on her mind. She didn't normally venture into the tree house. After a few minutes of niceties like 'How are you?' and 'What are you drawing?' Peggy mustered up enough courage to ask Rosie if there was something she wanted to talk about. As Peggy had guessed, there was. It turned out that Rosie had met a lad where she worked and he had asked her if she would like to go to the picture house with him to watch the latest film that Saturday night. Peggy was impressed. 'What, you mean out on a *date*?'

'Yes of course!' replied Rosie with a hint of sarcasm in her voice.

'Wow, how exciting!' Peggy exclaimed. 'What does your mum think? What are you going to wear?'

'Well, that's the problem,' said Rosie. 'I haven't told Mum or Dad yet. I'm scared of what they'll say. This will be my first ever date and I really like

Archie. I'm worried that as they don't know him, they won't let me go.'

Peggy thought for a moment. 'I've got an idea,' she said. 'What about talking to my mum first about it, or let me, and then maybe she could talk to your parents?'

Rosie thought, and then thought some more. It wasn't quite what she had expected Peggy to say, but then she didn't really know what she'd thought Peggy would come up with when she first decided to confide in her.

A plan was hatched, and for Peggy and Rosie it meant the deepening of a friendship. Peggy was never quite sure what made Rosie confide in her all of a sudden, but the idea that Rosie didn't have any sisters made Peggy feel rather proud that she had been able to help.

The plan was a good one, and Rosie and Archie did indeed go to the picture house – but not before the Arnolds had invited Archie round for tea to get to know him.

War

They say if you lived through the Second World War you always remember where you were when you heard that England had declared war on Germany.

Peggy heard the news not by sitting with the rest of her family listening to the radiogram, but from her mother. She was sitting high up in the tree house when she spied her mother attempting to climb up the narrow ladder to the trap door. Her mother hated heights, so it was obvious to Peggy that something serious was up.

'Mum, what are you doing coming up here?'

'Well, I know how much you love it up here, so I thought rather than ask you to come down for a chat I would come up to you.'

'What do you want to chat about?' Peggy asked nervously.

'There's no easy way of saying this, Peggy love, but it has just been announced that Britain has declared war on Germany.'

'War, that's terrible ... But it won't really affect us

here, will it? I mean, the last war was mainly fought in France.'

Peggy noticed how her mum brushed her thumb over her wedding ring.

'So why are you looking so upset, Mum?'

Peggy's mother caught hold of her hand and said, 'If this war is anything like the last, many soldiers will go off to war and not come back. Or, come back but be physically or mentally scarred by the horrors they have witnessed. If it goes on for a long time, men in everyday jobs like your father and Stan will be needed to go and fight too. There will be some men that will want to join up before they are called to do so. Also, this war could be completely different, this time affecting all of us over here a lot more than you think.'

As Peggy started to understand how much war would have an impact on everyone, she looked up and saw the fear and sadness in her mother's eyes. Then it hit her. BANG! All of a sudden, the realization dawned on her. The fear that Peggy saw in her mother's face was there because she knew that her husband would want to go and join up.

At first the shock of her discovery made her heart pound and then, no matter how hard she tried not to cry, the tears came. They welled up in her eyes and just rolled down her face. Overwhelmed with panic, she threw her arms around her mother

43

and they held each other tight for a very long time.

What could her mother say to make her feel better? Nothing. They both knew that the inevitable would happen. Peggy's father, being the sort of person he was, would leave them and join in the war effort. They could not know how long he would be gone. That was what was most scary of all.

Despite feeling as though her world was about to fall apart, Peggy couldn't face going in to see her father. She knew she wouldn't be able to control her emotions and she didn't want to let Kitty or Jack see how upset she was and so upset them as well. So she decided to stay in the tree house, yet again preferring to be in her sanctuary. Only this time everything around her seemed to be tainted. All the happy memories she had seemed tinged with unbearable sadness. On the one hand, it was the only place she wanted to be; on the other hand, she wanted to be as far away from all this madness as possible.

But where else in the world would she be able to find everything she had enjoyed here? Since she had moved in, the tree house had been the pivot around which everything else in her world revolved. She had felt from the very start of erecting the tree house – no, earlier, from designing it – that she had a connection with it, a bond that grew each time she visited it. She knew it sounded silly. How could she have a bond with something that wasn't alive? But that was how she felt.

Letting her mind wander, she realized that it wasn't just the tree house but the tree as well that she loved. The beech tree stood tall and strong, its roots firmly in the ground, its beautiful red copper leaves bursting through every spring. Maybe it was the beech tree she had a bond with: after all, the tree was alive.

Farewells

Peggy stared at the clock on the mantelpiece as she sat at the table with her breakfast in front of her. She was transfixed by the hands of the clock, watching them move from one minute to the next. Deep down inside herself, she wished for time to stop – for everything to stay exactly as it was now in her world and for it not to change.

However, try as she might, time did not listen to her wish and kept on moving forward. She had dreaded this day since her father had told her exactly when he would be going off to war. Oblivious to the world around her, she was suddenly made aware of her surroundings when Kitty came and stood next to her, clapping her hands loudly. 'Stop day-dreaming, Peggy! You're going to make Dad late for his train.'

Taking her eyes off the ticking clock and glancing down at her breakfast, Peggy decided she wasn't hungry. She could hear the rest of her family in the hall putting on coats and shoes. She took a deep breath and with head down walked quickly past everyone to get her own shoes and coat.

She kept her head down for most of the walk to the station. She was almost embarrassed by her feelings: at her age, she shouldn't be such a baby! But she couldn't bring herself to join in with the chatter.

As they neared the station, Peggy's heart started to beat faster and harder. She tried to take deep breaths and keep calm, but the harder she tried the worse she felt. Dreading that she would burst into tears in front of everyone, which she feared would upset her father, she tried to empty her mind and become numb. When her father came closer to her to give her a hug, she took a step backwards and quietly muttered, 'Bye, Dad.'

Her father, understanding perfectly how she felt, gave her a long, loving look and said softly, 'Bye, Peggs. Look after your mum for me, and before you know it I'll be back home again.'

He picked up his bag and turned to walk to the train. Just as he opened the door and stepped inside, Peggy's feelings overwhelmed her and with tears streaming down her face she ran up to the door of the carriage. Her father stepped quickly back out and they threw their arms around each other. Peggy, holding her father tightly, sobbed, 'I'll think about you every day and I'll write too.'

'Me too, Peggs. Now, don't worry. I'll be all right.'

Hearing the station master's whistle, her father stepped back inside the train and closed the door. As the train began to move, Peggy waved. Then she started to walk alongside it, still waving. Wiping away the tears as fast as they fell, she started to run along the platform, trying to keep up with the moving train as it gathered speed. Her father, leaning out of the window waving, was moving further and further away from her and no matter how hard she tried to keep up, the train won and Peggy had to give in and stop. She had reached the end of the platform. She kept her eyes firmly fixed on the waving figure of her father until the train turned a corner and he vanished from sight.

Evacuation

Peggy walked home from school with Kitty, Jack, Freddie, Madeline and Evie in tow. Leaving Freddie and the girls at the garden gates of their own homes, the Forester children carried on up the road. As she opened the front door, Peggy was deep in thought about her father and where he might be and what he might be doing at that particular time. Kitty and Jack both ran straight upstairs, past Peggy, who could hear voices coming from the front room. Although the voices were soft, she recognized Mary's immediately.

Then Mary said in a louder voice, 'Goodness me! Is that the time? My Freddie will be wanting his tea … Goodbye, Elizabeth!' She hurried out past Peggy, scooping up Teddy on the way. 'Hello and goodbye, Peggy!' she called over her shoulder. Dot, whose voice Peggy could also hear, followed quickly behind.

Her mother walked into the kitchen and collected a wicker basket on her way out into the garden. Rationing had started on food and other essentials, but Peggy's mother had already started to grow many different varieties of fruit and vegetables before the war, so they didn't have to worry so much about it.

Peggy followed slowly. She knew something wasn't right, but was afraid to ask what it was in fear that it might be something to do with her father, something bad. But what had her mum, Mary and Dot been talking about?

Eventually, she mustered up enough courage. Preparing herself for the worst, she blurted out, rather louder than she had intended, 'What's happened to Dad? Is he going to be all right? Please tell me the truth – I'm old enough to handle it! I'm not a child, Mum!'

Her mother stood still and for a split second looked shocked to hear Peggy shouting at her in that way. However, the penny soon dropped and she put down the basket and the vegetables she had in her hands and hugged Peggy. 'What we were talking about has nothing to do with your dad. As far as I'm aware, he's perfectly fine, wherever he may be. Let's go inside and I'll explain everything.'

Once indoors, Peggy's mum told her about the evacuation of all the children from towns and cities, which were the areas more likely to get bombed. The government had come up with an idea to send all the children who lived in built-up areas away to safer places in the country or by the sea, to live until the war was over. When Peggy's mum saw the panic on her face she went up to her daughter and gave her a big hug and said, 'Although many children will be sent away, Mary, Dot and I have all decided that's not what we want to do.'

'I don't understand, Mum. Don't all children everywhere have to go?'

'It's not compulsory, Peggy, every parent has a choice whether to send their children away or not. The government are just advising that it may be safer for children if they are not living in and around cities which may be bombed.'

'Do you think a lot of children will be sent away?'

'Maybe, I'm not sure, Peggy love.'

'Well, if they are, what will happen about school?'

'I have already discussed with Mary and Dot that if your school closes, because there aren't enough children, then I will teach you all.'

'Really? Would you be allowed?'

'I don't see why not.'

Peggy initially felt relief. She didn't want to leave her mum or her home. But then it dawned on her that staying might be dangerous, and she was overwhelmed by dread. Would it be a decision that they would come to regret? Hopefully not. That feeling of fear only lasted for a moment, though, and was replaced once again with a strong sense of relief.

She knew that none of the children would want to be sent away from their homes, families and friends to live with strangers somewhere they didn't know. She thought of all the other children who would be shipped off somewhere else. Supposing they were to end up with a family who were cruel to them? What would they do? It didn't bear thinking about, and she decided then and there that whatever happened, her mother had definitely made the right decision.

The week arrived when many of Peggy's friends were to be sent to their temporary new homes. Some were her own age from school and some came from the area where she lived. That morning she had seen Sarah and James Cooper, who lived in the road that ran along the end of her road, walking with their parents to the train station, suitcases in hand. She was standing looking out of her mother's bedroom window when she spotted them. As she watched, Sarah happened to look up and noticed Peggy at the window. She smiled, but Peggy could see the sadness in her eyes.

Later that week, finding comfort once again in the tree house, she looked out of the small window and across the surrounding gardens. It was five o'clock on a Friday afternoon, and before the evacuation there would have been the sounds of children playing out in their gardens or streets. Instead, apart from Mary's and Dot's children, whose voices she could now pick out quite clearly, it was quiet.

Although she would never have wanted to be evacuated, she suddenly realized that she felt lonely and sad. She opened up her diary and started to write about the events and emotions of the past few days. Underneath it all, she felt that it was the end of how things had been and they would never be the same again.

A Day Out

Peggy woke with excitement in her heart. Today was the day when Rosie was to be fitted for her wedding dress. As Peggy was to be bridesmaid, it meant that she too would get a new dress. They were going to London to visit Monty the tailor, who was a very good friend of Mary's family. His daughter Edith was a dressmaker and had offered to make Rosie's and Peggy's dresses as a wedding gift. It meant that Peggy, Elizabeth, Mary and Rosie were all to go up to town for the day. They decided to make a special 'mother-daughter' outing of it, and after the fitting they were to go to one of the London tea shops. It was the most exciting thing that had happened in ages. Kitty, Jack, Freddie and Teddy were all spending the day with Dot and her girls.

Peggy got dressed in her best frock, a pretty dark red dress with a frilly cream neckline. She wore a red ribbon in her hair, which she wore up in a pigtail at the back.

Her mum came in with Jack. 'Hold out your hand!' she said, clasping something tightly in her right hand. Peggy frowned, not knowing what to expect, but put out her opened hand for her mother to drop whatever it was in her palm.

She looked down and gasped. It was her mother's favourite brooch – a bronze art deco lady holding her hands gracefully above her head. Her long flowing hair partially fell over her face as it dropped forward around her. Her dress, like her hair, wrapped itself gracefully around her slender legs, which came to a point at her toes.

Peggy was taken aback. Her grandmother had given it to her mother when she got married. It was the 'something new' part of the wedding rhyme, 'Something old, something new, something borrowed, something blue.'

Peggy didn't know what to say, so instead she threw her arms around her mum and gave a her big hug.

'It's to go on your coat,' said her mother. 'Something special for a special day.'

'You look beautiful, Peggy!' Jack said, smiling.

'Thank you, Jack,' said Peggy, beaming as she turned to look in the mirror, pinning the brooch to her dress.

'Come on, children, time to go,' called her mother.

Everyone hurried themselves and congregated in the hall. They were dropping Kitty and Jack off at Dot's on the way to the station.

'Everyone ready with everything you need?'

'Yes!' came the chorus.

'Good. Then let's go.'

Just as Elizabeth shut the front door, Jack yelled, 'I've forgotten Ernie! I left him in the tree house this morning when I was playing in there.'

Ernie was Jack's favourite and first bear he had ever had. He was given to him by his dad on the day he was born. As Ernie is short for Ernest his mum had decided that Ernie would be a fitting name. He went most places with Jack and was always there at bedtimes.

'We haven't got time to go back and get him now. We'll miss our train, Jack.'

'Maybe you can borrow one of Teddy's instead?' suggested Peggy.

'That's a good idea. Now, we really need to go,' their mother said, and she hurried them along the path. Jack reluctantly agreed and sauntered up the road behind them, hands in pockets.

After saying their goodbyes at Dot's house, Elizabeth and Peggy picked up Mary and Rosie, and hurried on to the station to board the train for London.

Although central London was only ten miles away, they hadn't ventured into the city since the war had started. It had become especially dangerous since the Germans had started their bombing blitz a few months earlier. Most nights London took a battering from the enemy. They would wait mainly until after dark so they couldn't be seen as easily. Sometimes, however, bombing raids were carried out before it got dark, which was one of the reasons why they hadn't been to London for such a long time. They would make sure they got home before dark, however.

Nothing was going to ruin the day for Peggy. She was determined to enjoy every minute – despite the rationing, the bombing, and the fact that the war had taken all their fathers away, which was especially sad for Rosie who would probably not have her father there on her special day.

She gazed out of the window most of the way, taking in all that she saw. With the rhythmic movement of the train she soon found herself day-dreaming and remembering how it had been before she moved. She hadn't realized how much she had missed going to London. Their old house had been much closer to the city and before they had moved and this wretched war had started, they would often visit London, taking a walk around Hyde Park or Regent's Park, or a stroll by the River Thames. The landmarks that made London famous for tourists were nothing special to Peggy, Kitty and Jack. This was their backyard, their home.

It wasn't until then that Peggy realized how lucky

she was to have had all that on her doorstep. Her memories were tinged with sadness. Not for the home she'd had, because she loved where they were living now, but because of the war. It made her feel as if they were in a kind of prison, denied their freedom to go wherever they wanted because of the dangers of being attacked. Children being sent away from their parents and families, food being scarce and rationed, fathers being sent away to fight and maybe die: all this made Peggy yearn for what life used to be like.

As they pulled into Waterloo Station, Peggy became aware of the conversation the others were having. Her mother was talking about the day she got married, and Mary was reminiscing about her own big day, Rosie listening with wide eyes.

They left Waterloo Station and headed for Monty's shop. The hustle and bustle of London excited Peggy and made her feel alive. There was something else, though, that Peggy could also sense as she walked – a feeling of hope and courage. People were just getting on with their lives, almost ignoring the fact that there was a war on, living with the knowledge that almost certainly there would be more bombing tonight, and if not tonight, then tomorrow. Maybe people felt they needed to just get on with it and carry on as usual, or maybe it was the way Peggy felt in her heart that made everything feel special.

The morning was spent with the girls choosing dress material and Rosie and Mary looking at wedding dress designs. They all knew how lucky the girls were to be having new dresses made, as everything was rationed and money was tight for everyone. So this experience was a real treat.

Before they left for home, they found a Lyons tea shop where they all had scones and tea served by a waitress dressed in a black-and-white uniform with her hair tied up in a bun. Peggy discovered that they were not called waitresses, but 'Nippies'. She had never seen a tea shop so huge. The vast room was impressive, especially to a fourteen-year-old girl. The glass chandeliers and cabinets glittered and shimmered as she walked past. The many lush green plants which were placed around the room all added to its splendour. Peggy was astounded by the number of small round tables, all decorated in crisp white tablecloths with a flower in a small vase in the middle of each.

Again, out came the diary, so that Peggy could write all about the tea shop. The Nippy who served them was particularly interested in Peggy's memoirs as she could see Peggy busily writing away. Peggy asked if she could sketch the waitress, and when the girl found out that Peggy was writing all about her experiences in London, including the tea shop and the waitress herself, she gasped and said admiringly, 'Well I never! Maybe I'll be famous one day when you're a successful writer and publish your memoirs.' Peggy grinned from ear to ear. She was so flattered that someone had taken an interest in her memoirs. Everyone she knew at home was so used to her writing in her diary that no one ever commented on it any more.

They were so busy talking and taking in the atmosphere of the place that all four of them forgot the time. It was only because their Nippy came over and asked if there was anything else they wanted, as she would soon be finishing her shift, that Mary looked at the huge black-and-white clock that hung between two gilded mirrors at the end of the room.

'Oh my goodness,' she gasped. 'Look at the time! We've been so busy nattering we'll miss our train!'

'Quick, girls, grab all your belongings!' Elizabeth said, as Mary hurriedly paid the Nippy.

Peggy was just placing her diary into her bag when they heard the all-too-familiar sound of the air raid siren. The unmistakable sound of the whirring siren, moving from low to high pitch, made everybody in the tea room stop momentarily, then all at once grab their belongings and hurry to the door.

'Where are we going to go for shelter, Mum?' Rosie said anxiously.

'We'll follow everyone else to the nearest Underground station,' replied Mary.

Fortunately, it wasn't far away. As the siren continued sounding its alarm, Peggy, Elizabeth, Mary and Rosie made their way down the many steps to the Underground. It was a new experience for them, not having been in central London during an air raid before. Back at home they used the large Anderson shelter in Dot's back garden. People with back gardens were encouraged to build a shelter. Families could go there during an air raid to help keep them safe from bombs being dropped. They were buried halfway down into the ground and made with metal sheets. Usually they were big enough for six people but Mr Potts had made a bigger one, so that's where Peggy and her family would go in an air raid. Peggy didn't like the shelter though. Like most, it was cold and damp and noisy when there was a bombing raid, which meant at night that you couldn't get any sleep.

Once they reached the station platform, they looked for some small space where they could all sit together for the duration of the bombing raid, however long that might be. There was no question of trying to get to Waterloo to catch a train home until the 'all clear' was sounded.

The first thing that struck Peggy was the sheer amount of people down there, many of whom seemed to have made the Underground their home. Entire families had brought along many essential items and a few home comforts.

She was stunned to see so many people all huddled together, just getting on with ordinary activities. Some were sleeping, others were drinking tea, there were quite a few reading and a couple of ladies were knitting. Many, though, were just chatting and laughing and there was even an old man right up the end of the platform playing his mouth organ. Peggy noticed that there was a table set up at one end of the platform serving refreshments, as if they were all there to watch some sort of show or be entertained. Many people had obviously been down there a while, judging from the amount of possessions they had with them, including kettles and gas burners to heat the water. There were makeshift beds all over the place, and in some of them small children were sleeping.

For the first time it dawned on Peggy that this was where many people came when they lost their homes through being bombed. They obviously had nowhere else to go. Although everyone was crammed in like sardines, the overall atmosphere was good. People seemed to be in good spirits. The worst thing was the din from the trains. Most of the stations were still in operation, including the one Peggy was in. Every so often a train would go whizzing past and some would stop to let people off. This would cause havoc, as the people getting off the train would have to step over others on the platform to get to where they were going.

Peggy got herself comfortable and opened her bag to get her diary out. She had just started writing when she heard a voice above her head. She looked up to see their Nippy from the tea room. 'That's dedication for you, all right, writing down here in this dingy light! I reckon you're going to be famous one day. You mark my words.'

They invited the waitress to sit down with them and thought it was about time they asked her name. It turned out that her name was Nora and she was from East London. She and her family now lived in Peckham. Nora had been born within the sound of Bow Bells, making her a true Cockney, something she was truly proud of. She lived with her mother, brother and grandmother in a two-up, two-down townhouse. Her father had died when she was young and that was when her Gran had moved in. They all talked for some time while overhead London took another battering from the bombers.

It was a couple of hours later when the air raid siren sounded again, this time to tell them the bombing had stopped and it was all clear.

When they emerged from the Underground, their first instinct was to look around to see what damage had been done. However, this time the bombers had obviously had their eye on other parts of London, as everything above ground where they were was still intact.

It was time for Nora and Peggy to go their separate ways. Nora suggested that they swap addresses and write to each other, which thrilled Peggy. She loved to write letters, but never really had anyone to write to, and receiving them would make her feel very grown up. Peggy continued to write about her experiences on their journey home, feeling that she had had the perfect day. Even the long wait in the Underground had been a fascinating experience. She hadn't felt so contented and full of hope since before the war, but it felt a lot longer than that. Ever since her dad had left them, she had felt anxious all the time and weighed down in her heart. She felt she had to be the responsible one out of her siblings, as she was the eldest, and had tried to help her mum whenever she could. She could see the tears of sadness in her mother's eyes at times when she thought that no one was watching, and could feel how pressured she felt to be positive all the time for the sake of everyone else. Even though no words had passed between her mother and herself about how Elizabeth felt with her husband away at war, Peggy knew that at night, as her mother lay in bed alone, the fear and sadness must overwhelm her. She knew because she felt the same.

Today, though, had given them all some much needed respite and brought some cheer and happiness to each one of them.

Coming out of the station where they lived, however, they immediately noticed that the surrounding area of their small town had been subjected to the wrath of the bombers. This wasn't unusual, as there was an aircraft factory nearby which had been targeted before. Also the enemy bombers would often drop their bombs up and down the railway lines. This was to cause as much disruption as possible. So, as they had a train station in their town, it was always plausible they could be hit.

As the crow flies, the aircraft factory was about a mile directly behind where they lived. It seemed that this time the factory had been hit. They could see smoke coming from that direction.

It would take them a good half hour to walk home. As they walked, they speculated about how much damage could have been done to the factory. It was only when they got nearer to their own road that they realized the bombs had fallen and hit houses around the area where they lived.

They started to run.

Peggy, already tired from their busy day, found it

hard to run as fast as she normally would. However, as she was the only one not wearing high heels, she was still the first to get to the end of their road. She could see immediately that something had happened at the other end. She paused for breath, then continued to run.

There were people everywhere. Some were her neighbours. As she ran, she glanced this way and that, searching for any signs of her brother and sister.

It was only when she neared the far end of her road that she stopped abruptly. The shock of what she saw would stay with her for the rest of her life.

Tears of Sadness, Tears of Joy

For a brief moment Peggy stood stock-still, unable to comprehend what her eyes were seeing. It was as if she was numb, devoid of any sense of hearing, touch or smell. It was as if she was watching everything on a big screen at the cinema: it was surely not real.

However, reality hit hard when she lurched out of her dream-like state to realize that the woman now standing across the road from her screaming for her children was Mary. Only hours before, they had been laughing together in a London tea shop.

It dawned on Peggy that a house in their street had been bombed, and that house belonged to the Potts, the very house where all of the children had been left that morning. All her senses came flooding back. Her heart started to pound in her chest with fear. Her mother was standing next to Mary, talking to a man in uniform, while a couple of neighbours were trying their best to hold Mary back from running into the wreckage of the house. Her mother seemed a lot calmer than Mary on the surface, but

Peggy knew it was just her way. Underneath her calm exterior, she would be frantic. It was obvious to Peggy, however, that she was trying to obtain all the information before assuming the worst.

Peggy walked slowly towards her mother, trying to brace herself for terrible news. She had no sooner reached her mother's side when she heard her name being shouted from behind. She whirled round to see Kitty, Freddie, Madeline and Evie standing in front of a man and a woman whom Peggy vaguely recognized.

Seeing the four of them standing there, she turned around and grabbed her mother's arm, yelling excitedly, 'They're OK! They're all OK, Mum! Look, Mary!'

They started to rush across the road to each other. Only then did Peggy notice that Jack and Teddy were not there. The others noticed too.

'Where are Teddy and Jack?' Mary demanded to know from Freddie as she grabbed him by the arms.

'And what about Mr and Mrs Potts?' Rosie said in a hesitant voice. If she didn't say it too loud, then maybe what she feared to be true wouldn't be true.

Everyone looked to each other for an answer. Then they turned back to the four children who stood before them.

It was Freddie who spoke up, timid and quiet. 'We

were all in the shelter where Mr Potts told us to go. Teddy was inside the house with Mrs Potts because he was tired. She took him inside to have a nap. Well, it all happened so quickly. We'd all been in the garden playing, including Mr Potts. When he heard the siren he told us all to run into the shelter while he called for Mrs Potts. The last we saw of him, he was heading for the house.'

'That must mean they were all in the house!' Mary sobbed, collapsing to the ground.

'What about Jack? Where was he?' Elizabeth asked, tears in her eyes.

'We don't know,' Freddie told her. 'Not long before we heard the bomb, he went off in a huff because he wanted us to climb over your gate to your back garden and get Ernie from the tree house.'

Peggy swung round to look at what was left of the Potts' house. Apart from a corner of the far left wall and part of what would have been Madeline's and Evie's bedroom floor, there was nothing. Everything else had gone. What was once a beautiful home was now rubble, dust and smoke. How could anyone still be alive under all that debris?

Suddenly, Peggy rushed over to Freddie, who was standing next to Rosie with a pale, emotionless face. 'Freddie,' she said urgently, 'what did you say happened with Jack before the bomb hit?'

Freddie turned his head slowly and lifted his eyes

to look at her. It was then that Peggy could see his face wasn't emotionless. Tears filled his eyes.

Peggy continued with her questions. She had to know. 'Can you remember how long before the bomb hit that Jack went off in a huff to look for Ernie?'

'Yes, a few minutes,' replied Freddie.

'What, two, five, ten minutes?' persisted Peggy.

'Maybe three or four minutes. Why?'

'Freddie, I need you to come with me now.' Peggy grabbed Freddie's arm and pulled him towards her.

'Where are we going?' he asked.

Peggy said nothing, but simply held on to Freddie's arm and ran towards her own house. When they got there, she asked Freddie to help her over the back gate. Once over the gate, she ran straight to the tree house, while Freddie tried to find something to stand on so he could see what was going on.

Peggy clambered up the steps to the tree house and pushed the trap door open. She peered in and looked around the room. At first she couldn't see anything unusual and her heart sank. Then, just as she was going to go back down the ladder, she saw the heap of blanket in the corner move.

'Jack!' she called out.

'Peggy, is that you?' came a wavering voice.

'Yes it is! Jack, you're alive!' Peggy burst through the opening to the tree house just as a frightened, tear-stained face appeared from under the blanket.

She threw her arms around her brother's tiny body and hugged him. Tears rolled down her face as she sobbed, 'I thought I was never going to see you again. How did you manage to get over the fence?'

'Next door's back gate was open, so I crept down their back garden and stood on their tree stump next to our fence and climbed over. The fence isn't that high there.'

There came a pause from Jack, and then he added, 'Peggy, am I in trouble for running away from the Potts' house to get Ernie? Only I was really scared when the bomb came. Everything shook – the whole tree and the tree house. I was too scared to move in case it fell out of the tree.'

'Absolutely not, Jack,' soothed Peggy. 'No one will be cross with you. Just the opposite. Everyone will be so pleased you're alive.'

Peggy knew that Jack didn't yet realize that the Potts' house had been bombed. How could he? He was already in the tree house when the bomb hit. She thought it better not to tell him until her mother had had a chance to see him and he had calmed down a bit. She called down to Freddie, who was still waiting patiently outside the gate, and told him to go and get her mother and tell everyone that Jack was alive and well.

Despite her shocked disbelief at what had just happened and the fear of what was yet to be discovered, Peggy felt an overwhelming sense of relief. Sitting there holding Jack tightly, she felt safe and secure. More than that, she felt a strength that she hadn't felt before. She felt sure it was coming from the tree house. At that moment she believed wholeheartedly that it was her safe haven and that it had always and would always be there for her. Whether it was in good times or bad times, the Elephant Tree House would be her sanctuary and she would never leave it.

Regrets

Darkness fell, but the rescue efforts continued as they tried to find everyone believed to be in the Potts' house when the bomb fell. Many people who lived in the surrounding area rallied round to help in one way or another. Most of the able men helped with lifting and passing pieces of rubble, charred wood and debris from the remains of the house, and every so often everyone was ordered to be quiet so they could listen for any sound coming from underneath the wreckage.

Everyone was so relieved when they discovered Jack was alive; it gave a boost to everyone's morale. Even Mary for a brief while believed that if one miracle could happen, then maybe a second was possible.

Then they discovered the body of Eric Potts.

A sombre silence fell amongst the men and women who were there helping as they carried his body across the road to an ambulance waiting to take survivors and non-survivors alike to the hospital. Both Madeline and Evie had been taken to a neighbour's house down the end of the street to be spared the sight of what might emerge from the rubble of their home. Peggy had waited with Rosie to keep her company, both girls wanting to be there in case there was any news.

Then, sometime late into the night, there came a shout from one of the rescuers asking for some help. They had found something or someone. Although now it was becoming more and more unlikely that they would find either Dot Potts or Teddy Arnold alive, people still hoped and prayed for a miracle. A neighbour had taken Mary indoors. By then she was in such a bad way she could hardly stand. Elizabeth had gone home to be with Kitty and Jack.

They had found Dot. Underneath her lay Teddy.

Neither had survived. There were to be no further miracles that night.

The discovery had left Madeline and Evie orphans, and Mary without her beloved Teddy. They carried Teddy away on a stretcher with a sheet covering his body. As he passed Peggy, she could make out his tiny form underneath the sheet.

The events of the day had left Peggy feeling she was living in a surreal world. She walked home once she realized there was nothing else she could do, feeling sick and drained. As she walked along the road she noticed how some of the houses had their windows blown out. Also the force of the explosion had meant there was debris from the Potts' house strewn across the road and in people's gardens. Strange how she had run past the debris without noticing when she was looking for Jack. It just added to her feeling of being completely devastated about what had happened. Once inside the house, she stopped at the door to her mother's bedroom. There lay Kitty and Jack, fast asleep, one either side of their mother. Elizabeth, who wasn't asleep, looked up to see Peggy standing there. Neither of them said anything. They didn't have to. Elizabeth could tell by Peggy's tear-stained face that the news wasn't good. Peggy walked on to her own bedroom and collapsed on her bed.

After what seemed like an age of trying to get to sleep, Peggy's mind wandered back to the day when her mother, Mary and Dot had decided not to evacuate the children. Her heart sank even further. If Teddy had been evacuated, he would still be alive. She knew in that instant that Mary and her mother must be thinking the same, but with a huge burden of guilt added to the sick, sinking feeling she was experiencing.

Grieving

During the first few days after the Potts house was bombed, Peggy hardly knew how to muster enough energy and enthusiasm to get out of bed. The shock and disbelief that Mr and Mrs Potts and tiny Teddy were dead kept going around in her head. The whole experience of the bombing was the first thing she would think of when she woke in the morning and the last thing in her head at night as she drifted into a disturbed sleep.

The rest of her family were also subdued and although they talked about what had happened, it was only in a practical way. They concentrated on helping with funeral arrangements, made sure Madeline, Evie, Mary, Rosie and Freddie were all right, and prepared meals for Mary so that she didn't have to worry about day-to-day chores. At times Peggy was almost overwhelmed by the grief, but whenever she looked at Jack she felt such relief to know that he was alive and that she could just hold and cuddle him whenever she wanted. This brought her a strange comfort, coupled with guilt.

How could she feel pleased about anything at a time like this? She felt all muddled up inside, not knowing whether to feel happy that Jack was alive or sad that Teddy and Mr and Mrs Potts were dead. She wanted to talk to her mother about it, but her mother was busying herself with helping Mary. Peggy got the distinct feeling that this was how her mother was coping with the tragedy and that she didn't want to talk about it – not yet, anyway. Usually her mother would be concerned first of all about how her children were feeling, but now she didn't give herself time to sit down for a moment.

If Peggy's family were feeling like this, then what must Rosie, Freddie, Madeline and Evie be feeling? It was too difficult for Peggy to comprehend. And how should she act towards them when she saw them next? It had only been a few days since the bombing, and as yet she hadn't been to see any of them. She had been helping her mother prepare meals for Mary and looking after Kitty and Jack when her mother was out, so she hadn't had the chance to visit any of her friends. This made her feel guilty, but also somehow relieved that she had an excuse for not going to see how they were. She couldn't help but feel that anything she said would be inadequate. Perhaps saying nothing would be better than saying the wrong thing. However, that didn't feel right either. In the end she decided that the best thing to do would be to face her fear and go and see them.

Fortunately for Peggy, Kitty wanted to go and visit them too. They decided to start with Madeline and Evie. She knew that having Kitty with her would help to break any awkward silences.

So, they walked down to the end of the road to where Mrs Baker lived, which was where the girls had been staying. Mrs Baker was well known in the street. Everybody loved her, she was a bit like everyone's granny because she was such a warm person. She never had a bad word to say about anyone and would be the first person in a crisis to offer genuine help. This was why the girls ended up staying there.

As soon as they entered Mrs Baker's house, Kitty went straight up to Madeline and Evie and gave them both a big hug. 'I'm so sorry,' she said simply.

Peggy decided to do the same. 'How are you?' she asked anxiously.

To her surprise, they seemed fine, more chatty than she thought they would be. Maybe they were still in shock and probably their loss hadn't really sunk in yet.

She was glad that she did go and visit them, though, as they had some news.

'We are so glad you came round to see us, I said to Evie this morning that if you hadn't come by this afternoon, maybe we should come and see you. We weren't sure how you were feeling after everything that had happened and thought that was probably why you hadn't come over yet,' Madeline explained.

Peggy felt very embarrassed that she had left it so long, even though she knew that's not what Madeline had intended to imply. However, her embarrassment was soon replaced by shock with what Madeline said next.

'We wanted to come and see you both before we left for Wales.'

'Wales! Why are you going there?' Peggy blurted out.

'We have an aunt and uncle who live there and they have offered to look after us from now on.'

'But Wales is such a long way … It won't be the same without you in this street,' Kitty said sadly. 'Why can't you stay here with Mrs Baker?'

'We couldn't expect Mrs Baker to look after us forever. She's elderly and it wouldn't be fair when we have relatives who can take us in. We know Wales is a long way but we don't have a choice, there is no one else.' Madeline walked over to Kitty and gave her a big hug.

'When are you going?' asked Peggy.

'The day after tomorrow,' replied Madeline.

Peggy and Kitty gave each other a tearful look

and Peggy said, 'We'll miss you. Please write to us, won't you? And we promise we will write back. We must stay in touch.'

Madeline and Evie agreed.

Peggy left the house with an overwhelming urge to turn back and ask them if there really wasn't anyone else they could live with here. She knew this was a purely selfish thought: she would miss them dreadfully. All the children in the street had become like one big happy family. Now, with Teddy gone and Madeline and Evie moving away, Peggy felt as if her world was falling apart again. She had felt the same when her dad left. She wanted to run across the road to her tree house and stay there, hoping that her sanctuary would somehow calm her down and make the sadness go away. She and Kitty looked at each other as they crossed the road. Peggy could tell that Kitty felt the same sadness. Madeline had become one of her best friends.

They knew that they had to continue with their plan and go on to visit Mary, Rosie and Freddie. Peggy was dreading this more. The last time she had seen Mary, she had been totally distraught. Peggy had never seen anyone that upset before. Even though she understood why, she was still concerned. What if either Kitty or Peggy said something with the best intentions but upset Mary? Peggy didn't think she could handle that. Then she remembered that Rosie would be there to help, and her worry lifted a little.

When they arrived, Rosie answered the door looking pale and tired. She took them through to the kitchen where they could talk quietly, as her mother was sleeping in the lounge, the first time in a while. Peggy suddenly felt very selfish and guilty for worrying about how *she* would cope with Mary being upset.

Freddie came in a few moments later and sat down at the kitchen table. At first no one said anything but then, not being able to stand the awkwardness, Peggy said, 'Have you heard about Madeline and Evie moving to Wales?'

Rosie and Freddie glanced over at each other.

'Why Wales?' Freddie asked curiously.

'They have family there, an aunt and uncle. They're leaving in two days,' Peggy explained.

'That's soon, but I suppose there is no point in leaving it any longer. They probably just want to be able to get settled somewhere and to be able to grieve properly. Anyway, it's probably for the best as they wouldn't really want to carry on living in the area, seeing where their old house was. It would be a constant reminder of what happened,' Rosie replied.

Peggy hadn't thought of it that way but she agreed.

They were discussing both the girls moving away when Peggy glanced over at Rosie. She could see tears welling up in her eyes and could tell Rosie was fighting them back. Should she ask if Rosie was all right? Should she go over to her? Or should she just pretend that she hadn't really noticed? *I'm no good at this sort of thing!* she thought desperately.

Just then Kitty got up and walked over to Rosie. 'I'm so sorry about Teddy!' she said, throwing her arms around Rosie and hugging her.

Peggy mentally kicked herself. She should have been the first to do that! She got up to move round the table and hug Rosie herself, but then she noticed that Freddie had his head buried in his arms, obviously not wanting to show anyone how upset he was. Without thinking or worrying about what was the right thing to do, she went up to him, stooped down and gave him a hug. 'Everyone will miss Teddy,' she told him gently.

Later that day Peggy went up into the tree house. She just sat there at first, looking out of the tiny window, hoping to feel some sort of comfort that would make her believe everything was going to be all right. It didn't come.

It occurred to her that she hadn't written anything in her diary since before the bombing. It was where she had left it, placed on the upside-down wooden box that she had made into a table. She had put it there a couple of days after the bombing intending to try and write her thoughts down. However, she found she could not find the words inside herself to describe how she felt so she had left it there hoping soon she would be able to. She reached over and opened it to her last entry. Reading about how excited she had felt to be in London and everything that she had experienced that day in town made her want to turn the clock back, to try to change the awful way that day had ended.

If they hadn't gone to London and had stayed at home instead, then things would have been so different. Yes, the house would still have been bombed, but Mrs Potts would not have been indoors looking after a sleeping Teddy, and Mr Potts would not have gone in to get them. All the 'what ifs' going around her head made it throb.

She sat there looking at the words she had written, picking out certain ones that portrayed how happy she had felt that day before they arrived home. She wondered if she would ever be able to put into words how she felt about the events of that day. Then it occurred to her that if she went through her diaries, she could pick out all the things she had written that included Teddy. Her diaries were written memories. Maybe Peggy's memories could help comfort Mary in some way? Perhaps not now, but later, when she was more able to deal with what had happened.

So Peggy set about re-reading her diaries and decided to make a little story about Teddy. She included things that she remembered along the way that weren't in any of the diaries. It was strange how reading about all the things that she and her friends had done brought back to mind far more than she had actually written down. As she worked, she realized that making this book of memories about Teddy was already helping her to understand how she felt about everything that had happened.

The Date

The funerals of Mr and Mrs Potts and Teddy came and went. The days turned into weeks, and the weeks into months. Life went on. It was hard at first, but getting back to some kind of normality – if you can call living through a war 'normal' – helped Peggy with her grieving.

Madeline and Evie left the street to go and live with their aunt and uncle in Wales, and at first the street felt empty. Also, Rosie had decided to postpone her wedding for a while. Weddings were supposed to be a happy occasion and she didn't feel happy at all. She decided the best thing would be to give herself and everyone else some time to come to terms with Teddy's death. Everyone understood. However, it meant that the five children who were left were brought closer together. For two of them, a special friendship started to flourish. It had been obvious from the start that Freddie had a soft spot for Peggy. Recent events had brought them even closer together.

Because their little gang had decreased in

numbers, the children who were left in the street spent more time together as a whole group. They would do lots of things together, such as going to Saturday morning cinema. On one such occasion Peggy, Freddie, Kitty and Jack had arranged to go and watch the latest film. When the day arrived, however, Kitty and Jack were both ill with colds, so just Peggy and Freddie went.

While they watched the usual Pathé newsreel about the troops and the war, Peggy kept finding herself thinking about her father. Where was he? Was he all right? All of a sudden she had a strange feeling in her stomach.

They had watched the Pathé newsreels often, and Peggy had never been affected like this before. However, she just couldn't shake the uneasy feeling she had – a sense of dread washing over her. Feeling as if she couldn't breathe, she panicked, leapt up and rushed out of the cinema. Freddie raced after her, not knowing what was going on. He found her in the lobby of the cinema with tears welling up in her eyes.

'What's the matter, Peggy? Are you ill?'

Peggy said nothing. She didn't know how to explain.

'Do you want to go home?' Freddie asked. Peggy nodded.

Neither of them said anything as they walked home, but a few minutes after they left the cinema,

Peggy felt Freddie's hand catch hold of hers. Her first reaction was to pull away from him, but she stopped herself and instead turned towards him and smiled. He smiled back.

When they reached Peggy's house, Freddie broke the silence. 'Are you feeling better?'

'Yes, thanks,' she said.

They said their goodbyes, and just as Peggy was opening the gate, Freddie turned back and said quickly, 'How do you fancy going to the pictures next Saturday – just the two of us?'

Peggy hesitated, then smiled. 'OK,' she said shyly.

Freddie had the biggest grin on his face that Peggy had ever seen. He waved and said, 'Great! See you tomorrow …' before running down the road to his house.

Peggy went straight up to the tree house. She sat there trying not to think about how she had felt in the cinema. Instead she thought about Freddie asking her to the pictures the following Saturday. She knew it was going to be a date, but it didn't bother her. It would have embarrassed her a while ago. Now, though, she just felt happy about it. She was growing up. Also, because it was Freddie she was going with, she knew she wouldn't feel awkward. It would just be like when they all went together and because they had become so much closer, she trusted him.

She wished now she had told him about how she felt in the cinema. She knew he would have understood, but she didn't really want to acknowledge that feeling of dread, like something bad was looming, especially after the bombing. There had been a lot of bombing going on in and around London since the beginning of the war. Many people had lost their lives and their homes. It was hard for everyone and everyone had to pull together. It was especially hard, though, if you knew the victims and were close to them. Maybe it was a delayed reaction to everything that had happened and was still happening around London and England. Maybe she was scared that it wasn't ever going to stop, and if it did it might not end well. She never usually let herself think like this. However, her panic in the cinema had unnerved her. She started writing in her diary about the date with Freddie, and about her nagging doubt that something unpleasant was going to happen.

The week went by uneventfully and Saturday morning arrived. Peggy got up early and helped her mother with some chores. She then went upstairs and got dressed. She was just trying to fix a hair clip when she heard a knock at the front door. Kitty rushed to open it and then called up to Peggy, 'Your boyfriend's here!' Giggling, she ran off, leaving Freddie standing red-faced at the door.

'Take no notice of Kitty!' said Peggy's mother cheerfully, coming out of the kitchen to greet Freddie.

Peggy came down and rushed out of the door past her mother, calling over her shoulder, 'See you later!'

Her mother had no time to say anything except 'Have a good time!' to their retreating figures. Peggy and Freddie enjoyed the film and took a slow walk home. Peggy was relieved that she was able to watch the film this time without any odd feelings making her feel uneasy. As she walked home she decided to tell Freddie how she had felt the week before – when she had run out of the cinema without an explanation.

'Freddie … I'm sorry about what happened last week, when I ran out and left you.'

'That's OK, Peggy, it doesn't matter.'

'Thank you, Freddie, but I just wanted to explain. Watching the Pathé news reminded me about how much I miss my dad and just wish I knew he was all right and going to come home soon. I know I am not the only one to be missing someone who's fighting in the war, you must miss your dad all the time too. It's just … well I had this overwhelming feeling that something bad had happened to him. Anyway I was thinking after, it was probably just delayed shock or something.'

'I've never had anything like that happen to me, Peggy, but it sounds like you're probably right. I am sure both our dads are OK.'

'Yes, I'm sure. Anyway, I feel better now.' Peggy glanced over at Freddie and gave him a smile.

When they got back to Peggy's house, she asked Freddie if he wanted to come in and hang out in the tree house for a while. They walked into a relatively quiet house and couldn't hear anything at first. But then, as they walked along the hallway past the closed living room door, Peggy heard what she thought was crying.

She took hold of the handle and slowly opened the door. Looking back towards Freddie, she could see that he shared her apprehension. He gave her a little encouraging nod. Peggy crept into the room and found her mother, Kitty and Jack. Jack was kneeling on the floor playing with his toy wooden train. Kitty was sitting sobbing on the sofa, cuddled up to their mother, who had her eyes shut and was repeating the words, 'Everything is going to be all right. You'll see.'

At first Peggy thought Kitty had hurt herself in some way and her mother was comforting her. However, as she entered the room she had a strong feeling that something else was wrong. The whole atmosphere felt strange. Then she noticed the opened letter on the small table next to the sofa and her heart started to pound. She looked again at Freddie, who had followed her into the room. He looked as bewildered and worried as she felt.

'Mum, what's wrong?' Peggy asked tentatively.

Peggy's mother opened her eyes and looked bleakly at her elder daughter. Tears welled up and began to fall down her face. Peggy was at once overtaken by that same feeling of dread that she had experienced at the cinema the week before. Heart hammering, she almost wished she hadn't asked the question. She knew she didn't want the answer.

Peggy's mother picked up the letter. 'A telegram was delivered while you were out. It's about your father.'

She stood up and walked over to Peggy with her arms outstretched, as if about to hug her. All at once Peggy started to tremble and felt her cheeks becoming wet with her own tears. She took the sheet of paper from her mother's hand. Her eyes quickly skimmed the words of the telegram: 'ERNEST FORESTER … MISSING IN ACTION …'

Peggy ran from the living room, through the house and out into the garden. She frantically climbed the ladder to the tree house and threw herself down on the large cushion. Pulling her knees up tight to her chest, she wrapped her arms around her legs, buried her head, closed her eyes tight and started to sob uncontrollably.

Desperately, she wished herself away from this time and place, to a happy time before the war. All of a sudden she felt the warmth of an arm around her and heard the words, 'Don't fret, Peggy, don't fret,' said in a quiet and gentle way. She looked up to find not the face of her mother, but the face of Freddie. Her friend, who had become her best friend.

Present Day

Jessica read every page of every diary avidly, completely captivated by each entry and compelled to read on until she had finished them all.

From the start she felt drawn into Peggy's world, to life in the 1930s and 1940s. She would occasionally try to talk to her parents about the fascinating stories in the diaries, but although they were happy about her restored enthusiasm for reading, they weren't really interested in the tales she had to share. All their time and energy was spent doing up the house, and so Jessica was left alone with her stories.

She would often stop and look around her bedroom and think about the old lady Peggy had become and how sad it was that she had died alone here, probably with no family around her. Jessica would have loved to meet her. She knew that was impossible, so she would read Peggy's last diary entry and try to imagine what else happened in her life.

9th May 1945

What a glorious day we had yesterday, finally the end of the war. It seemed that as soon as it was announced everyone was celebrating. In central London apparently hundreds of thousands of people took to the streets, cheering and partying. Here in our street we had an impromptu party, everyone came. I can't remember seeing everyone so happy. Even Mum came and I could see how some of the stress had lifted from her face and she looked more relaxed than I had seen her in a long time. I think she's hoping that now the war is over maybe our beloved father will return as he is still officially missing in action. There is still hope in her heart that maybe, if he is a prisoner of war, now the war is over he will return home to us. I know that we all hope that will be the case although the rest of us are more realistic. The chances that he has been a prisoner all this time are slim and I don't want to get my hopes up. Things have not been the same since the day we received that telegram.

I can't believe that it has been so long since my last entry but what with looking after Mum and working, I just don't get the time. I remember a time when I wrote in it nearly every day and couldn't wait sometimes to run *up to the tree house and write. I must try every day to find time to make an entry.*

Anyway, better finish up for today as I can hear Jack teasing Kitty and by the sounds of it she's not happy. I'd better go and sort them out.

Jess felt sad when she read Peggy's last ever entry. She obviously had intended to write more but for some reason never got around to it. So Jess resigned herself to just having to imagine what happened.

One hot and sunny morning just at the beginning of the summer holidays, Jessica's mum wanted her to go out the front with Emily and watch her while she rode her bike up and down the street. Emily wasn't that confident yet on her bike and would frequently fall off.

After a while of cycling up and down outside their house, Emily wanted to cross over and ride on the other side of the street. Jessica agreed to cross over with her and keep an eye on her sister while Emily tried desperately to keep both feet on the pedals for more than a few seconds at a time.

It was while Emily was managing her longest stint on her bike all morning that a car pulled up outside one of the houses and stopped. Seeing someone opening the car door as she approached unsteadily on her bike, Emily panicked and braked suddenly, falling off her bike with a thud.

'Emily!' called Jessica, running up. 'Are you all right?' She tried to untangle Emily from the bike. The people from the car came to help – an elderly man and a young girl about the same age as Jessica.

She and Jessica helped a sobbing Emily up off the pavement and sat her down on the wall behind them. The elderly man picked up the bike. 'That was a nasty fall,' he said, 'but I don't think you've broken anything. You'll just need a plaster for that cut knee.'

'Shall I go and get one from your first-aid kit, Granddad?' offered the girl.

'That's a good idea, Lucy. Here's the front-door key.'

As Lucy ran up the garden path of the house behind the wall Emily was sitting on, the old man decided to introduce himself to the two girls. 'My name's Fred,' he said cheerfully. 'What are your names?'

Jessica and a now much calmer Emily told him their names and said they had not long moved into the house with the 'Sold' sign still outside.

'Oh, you mean Miss Forester's old house?'

'Yes,' said Jessica enthusiastically. 'Did you know her?'

'Yes, very well,' Fred replied.

Just then the girl came running back carrying a

transparent plastic box. 'Here you go, Granddad,' she said breathlessly.

As Fred popped a plaster on Emily's gashed knee, he introduced Lucy, his granddaughter. It turned out that Lucy spent a lot of time at her granddad's house in the summer holidays, as her parents both worked. As they all walked up the road to Jessica's and Emily's house with Fred carrying the bicycle, the two older girls started chatting about school and which one they were going to, as there were several in the area to choose from. It turned out that Lucy was going to the same one as Jessica, but because all of Lucy's friends were going to different schools, she wouldn't know anyone else on her first day either.

They approached the house and Emily, feeling much better now, ran up and opened the front door, calling for her mum and dad. Both parents came to the door to see what was up as Emily explained about her accident. While they both thanked Fred and Lucy for their help, Jessica was bursting to ask Fred about Peggy and tell him about the diaries.

As he and Lucy turned to leave, Jessica blurted out, 'Would you like to see our tree house?'

While Lucy nodded enthusiastically, Fred replied, 'You decided to keep the tree house, then? It's been here for so long, I'm surprised there's any house left!'

'We didn't have much choice,' Jessica's dad told him. 'Both girls set their hearts on it.'

They walked through the house and into the garden, and when Fred saw the tree house, he exclaimed, 'Oh, I see you've smartened it up a fair bit! I remember when the Foresters first built it.'

'You lived here in the street when it was first built?' Jessica asked, curious to know who Fred was and how old he would have been at the time. Then, as Fred explained, the penny dropped and she realized that the old gentleman was Freddie himself! Excitedly, Jessica fired question after question at poor old Fred, who didn't know where to start first. She told him about the diaries that she found and asked him if he would like to see them. However, the burning question on her mind was to ask him about Peggy and what she was like before she died. Sensitively she broached the question, and was completely surprised by the answer.

'Oh no,' Fred told her. 'It wasn't Peggy who lived here. It was Kitty – she lived here the whole of the rest of her life, and died here too. Peggy's still very much alive!'

Jessica was stunned. Having found the diaries, she had assumed that the old lady who died here was Peggy. She had clearly put two and two together and come up with the wrong answer! Her first reaction was to be pleased that Peggy was still alive, but then she started to feel guilty about feeling relieved that it was Kitty and not Peggy. However, she couldn't help but feel that she had a bond with Peggy because of the diaries.

Fred explained that Peggy and Kitty had had some sort of falling out when they were young, after the war was over. Apparently, their father never returned from the war. He remained 'missing in action'. This was something Elizabeth, Peggy's mother, found extremely hard to cope with. She would say it was worse that he was missing, because if she knew he was dead she could grieve properly. This way she always hoped that maybe he would turn up one day. Over the weeks and months that passed after the war had ended, Elizabeth slowly became worse and worse, fading away into her own world, not aware of the real world around her, longing for her husband to walk through the door and for life to continue as it had been before he left.

It soon became apparent that someone needed to care for her. It was always assumed that Peggy, being the oldest, would do this. In fact, she agreed to do so for a while as Kitty had the chance to go and work in France as a seamstress for a well-known fashion retailer in Paris. This was something that Mary and Stan's tailor friends in London had arranged. However, it so happened that Peggy had also been offered a job. She had been working for a local newspaper, as a secretary at first, but as she got to know the editor more she finally plucked up enough courage to show him some articles she had written on various topics. He felt she showed a lot of promise and would occasionally let her write for the local paper. It was when a colleague of her boss from America came to visit that things really changed for Peggy. The colleague was an editor for an American newspaper. Her boss had shown him a couple of articles Peggy had written and he said that her style of writing was just what he was looking for in the new magazine he was going to launch. He approached Peggy and asked whether she would like to fly over to the States for six months and write some articles for this new magazine. Peggy knew that this would be a great opportunity for her. However, she was concerned that she was abandoning her family.

There were lots of discussions and finally Kitty said that as it was only for six months, maybe she could wait and go to Paris in six months' time if her future employers didn't mind.

Everything was sorted out and Peggy ended up going out to the States while Kitty looked after their mother. But six months became nine months, then another six months, then another year. In the end everyone knew that Peggy wasn't intending to come back. Kitty never forgave Peggy for not being honest with her and messing up her opportunity to fulfil her dream of going to France. She hadn't intended to stay in France for more than a year, just long enough to learn the trade so she could come back and get a good job in England. Then she could have taken over their mother's care once again. Unfortunately, in time the position in Paris had to be given to someone else. Those opportunities didn't happen very often, so Kitty missed out. She did eventually become a dressmaker, but not on the same scale as she had wanted, and it took her a long time to achieve her dream, especially as she was left with the responsibility of looking after her mother for many years. It also got in the way of relationships, as her mother always had to come first. So Kitty was bitter, and when Peggy tried to make amends by apologizing and sending money over to help, Kitty didn't want to know and sent the letters and money back.

Jessica was very much saddened by the story Fred told, and it dawned on her that Peggy had never been back to the house and the elephant tree she had loved so much. *If it had been me*, she thought, *I would have loved to come back and see it all again.*

Jessica looked over at the tree house and then back to Fred. 'Where is Peggy now?' she asked.

'Not far from here,' said Fred. 'Living with her

daughter and family. She's not well, though, which is why she decided to come back to England and live out her days here.'

'Could we go and see her and maybe invite her to come here one day?' Jessica asked nervously.

Fred paused, thought, then looked at Jessica with a smile. 'That would be a lovely idea, if Peggy's up to it.'

Memories and Friendships

The day Jessica had been waiting for finally came. She awoke with excitement and nervousness mixed together. Peggy was coming back to her family home. Jessica wondered if she would be able to remember any stories to tell them that were not in the diaries. However, she feared that Peggy was maybe too frail now to remember anything from her past, or that the visit would be too upsetting, bringing back memories she would rather forget. But then Jessica told herself that Peggy would have said 'no' to coming if she felt that way. One good thing that had come out of all this was that she had become very good friends with Lucy and was less scared of starting a new school after the summer holidays.

She busied herself with making sandwiches for lunch, and Emily helped with putting fairy cakes on plates. Then the knock on the door came and Jessica rushed into the hall, but stopped abruptly, feeling apprehensive. Emily overtook her and was therefore the first to greet the guests.

Peggy had come with her daughter and son-in-law. She was not much taller than Jessica herself, with a slight hunch in her back. Her hair was silvery grey and her eyes twinkled. The guests smiled at Emily and introduced themselves to Jessica's parents. Then lastly Jessica came forward and said shyly, 'Hello, I'm Jessica.'

Just at that moment, Fred and Lucy came in, Fred making his excuses for being late. Peggy made her way towards Jessica and caught hold of her hand. 'So this is the young lady who has become so fascinated with my diaries!' she said.

'Yes, this is who we all have to thank for today,' Fred replied.

'I am so pleased that someone had as much pleasure in reading them as I had in writing them,' said Peggy, smiling.

As it was such a lovely summer's day and Jessica was so keen to show Peggy the elephant tree and new tree house, everyone ventured out into the garden.

Peggy eyes lit up as she stepped into the garden and looked up at the tree house. Giving a little gasp of delight, her eyes suddenly welling up with tears, she turned to Jessica and caught hold of her hand again. 'Thank you so much for inviting me over today. I never thought I would see this place again. Out of all the homes I have lived in over the years, this one still has a special place in my heart.'

At that moment all Jessica's fears vanished. She knew that she had done the right thing. Peggy sat down next to Jessica on the garden bench and the pair talked and talked as if they were old friends linked together by stories of the past.

They chatted until Jessica could see that Peggy was becoming tired. 'I'll let you rest a bit,' she said, and climbed up into the tree house to play for a while with Emily and Lucy.

As Peggy watched them play and her eyes became heavy with tiredness, she let her mind wander back to her own childhood. The sound of Jessica's, Emily's and Lucy's laughter reminded her of her own good friends of all those years ago. As her eyes closed, there they all were: Kitty, Jack, Freddie, Rosie, Madeline, Evie and, of course, Teddy, just like it was yesterday, all laughing, singing, shouting, joking, playing happily together in and around the Elephant Tree.